Every new generation of children is enthralled by the famous stories in our Well-loved Tales series. Younger ones love to have the story read to them. Older children will enjoy the exciting stories in an easy-to-read text.

Published by Ladybird Books Ltd Loughborough Leicestershire UK
Ladybird Books Inc Lewiston Maine 04240 USA

Tiffany Barton

The Golden Goose

retold for easy reading
by BETTY EVANS

illustrated by FRANK HUMPHRIS

Ladybird Books

Once upon a time, there was a man who had a wife and three sons.

They all lived in a cottage on the edge of a forest.

The youngest son was called Simpleton, and everyone laughed at him because he wasn't as clever as his brothers.

One day the oldest son had to go into the forest to cut firewood. It would take a long time, so his mother gave him a cake and a bottle of wine for his mid-day meal.

When he came to the forest, the oldest son met a little grey man.

"I am so hungry and thirsty," said the little grey man. "Please will you give me a little piece of your cake, and a sip of your wine?"

"Certainly not," answered the oldest son. "If I give you any, I shall have nothing left for myself. Go away."

He began to chop at a big tree with his axe.

Soon the axe slipped and cut his arm,
and he had to go home to have it bandaged.

So the second son went into the forest to fetch the wood. His mother gave him a cake and a bottle of wine for his mid-day meal, just as she had given his brother.

Once again the little grey man appeared, and asked for a piece of cake and a sip of wine.

The second son was as selfish as the oldest son.

"If I give you any, I shall have less for myself," he said. "Go away and don't bother me."

In the same way as his brother, he was quickly punished for being so mean.

For, as soon as he began to chop, the axe slipped and cut his leg. He had to limp home without any wood.

"Father," said Simpleton, "why not let me go and cut the wood?"

"Oh no," said his father. "You know nothing about using an axe or working in the forest. Both your older brothers have hurt themselves. It would be asking for trouble to let you go as well."

"Please, father, let me go," said Simpleton again. "I'm sure I could do it."

At last his father said that he could go, and Simpleton set off. All he could take with him was some stale bread and a bottle of sour beer. There was no cake or wine left in the house.

As soon as Simpleton came to the forest, the little grey man met him.

"I am so hungry and thirsty," he said. "Please will you give me a piece of your cake, and a sip of your wine?"

"I'm sorry," said Simpleton, "there is only stale bread and sour beer. You may share those with me if you wish."

When they sat down to eat together, Simpleton found that the stale bread had turned into rich cake, and the beer had changed into wine.

After they had eaten, the little grey man said, "As you have shared your meal with me so willingly, I will reward you."

He pointed to one of the trees. "Chop down that tree there," he said, "and you will find something that will bring you good luck."

Simpleton picked up his axe and set to work to chop down the special tree.

When it fell he saw, sitting amongst the roots, a beautiful Golden Goose. It had feathers of purest gold.

Simpleton picked the goose up very carefully. Then instead of going home, he set out for a nearby inn to stay for the night. Before he went to bed himself, he put the goose safely to bed in a barn.

The landlord of the inn had three daughters. When they saw the goose, each of them longed for one of the golden feathers.

The oldest went to the barn first and tried to pull out a feather. Then she found that she was unable to let go!

When the other two sisters came they tried to help. But as soon as they touched their sister, they stuck fast to her. All three had to spend the night in the barn, stuck to the goose and to each other.

The next morning Simpleton came in, tucked the goose under his arm, and set out. He didn't seem to notice the three girls who were still unable to let go of the bird or each other. They had to follow him.

They were still tripping and stumbling along after Simpleton when they met a priest. He told them it was naughty to run after Simpleton like that and tried to stop them. But he too became firmly fixed and had to go with them.

As they went through the village, the sexton was amazed to see the priest following Simpleton and the three girls.

He called out to the priest, "Don't forget you have a christening this afternoon," and caught at the sleeve of the priest's coat. Then he too stuck fast and had to follow the others, willy nilly.

They all went on together, following Simpleton and the golden goose, until they saw two peasants digging in a field.

"Help us," shouted the priest and the sexton together.

The two men dropped their shovels and rushed up to help. They tried to pull the others away, but they too stuck fast.

There were now seven people in the little procession, all firmly stuck fast to the golden goose. Simpleton went happily on his way carrying the goose. He didn't seem to notice anything unusual.

Simpleton wasn't sure where he was going. He just kept on walking, his lucky goose tucked safely under his arm.

Over hill and dale, across fields and moors, he went with his goose. Through towns and villages they went, where people stared in wonder at them and their little band of followers.

At last, near the end of the day, they saw a great city on top of a hill.

Simpleton decided to go to the city, and
the little procession, of course, had to go
with him.

Now in this city reigned a king with one daughter. This princess was so serious that she never laughed and, because of this, the whole city was sad and gloomy.

The king was very worried about his daughter. He declared that whoever made her laugh could marry her and become a prince.

As Simpleton came near to the city, he heard of the king's promise. So he led his little procession straight to the Palace.

The princess, who looked very sad, sat gazing down from a window.

No sooner did the princess see Simpleton, the goose, and his seven weary followers than she began to laugh. Indeed, she laughed and laughed and laughed as though she would never stop.

The laughter of the princess broke the magic spell that had held the followers fast to the golden goose. They at once set out on their way home.

Simpleton, still clutching the golden goose, went straight to the king and asked for his reward, the princess as his bride.

The king was very happy to see his daughter laugh, but he didn't want her to marry a ragged woodcutter like Simpleton.

"Not so fast," said the king. "First you must bring me a man who can drink all the wine in my cellar."

Simpleton thought at once of the little grey man and set out for the forest. There, on the very spot where he had found his golden goose, he saw a stranger, looking very sad.

"What's the matter?" asked Simpleton.

"I'm so very, very thirsty," said the stranger.

"I think I can help you," said Simpleton. "Come with me and you shall have a whole cellarful of wine to drink."

They went to the king's palace, and the stranger sat down and began to drink and drink and drink.

Before the sun set that day, every barrel in the king's cellar had been drained dry. Once more Simpleton went to the king to claim his bride.

"No," said the king, who still did not want his daughter to marry this simple boy. "Now you must bring me a man who can eat a whole mountain of bread in one day."

Wasting no time, Simpleton went straight back to the same place in the forest. This time he found a man complaining bitterly that he was very, very hungry—even though he had already eaten an ovenful of loaves.

When he heard this, Simpleton was very pleased. He said, "I think I can help you. Come with me and you shall have a whole mountain of bread."

Back they went to the palace. The king's bakers had taken all the flour in the city and made so much bread that it stood like a mountain in front of the palace.

The man from the forest did not wait to be given a chair, or even a plate. He began to eat, still standing up.

He ate steadily, one loaf after another, while the people of the city gathered to stare and marvel at his appetite.

Sure enough, as the sun began to set, he finished the last crumbs, said ''Thank you'' to Simpleton—and vanished.

Simpleton went once again to the king and claimed his bride for the third time.

Once again the king refused. This time he said, "You must bring me a ship which can sail over both land and sea. Only then will I give you my daughter."

Yet again Simpleton set out for the forest, and this time met the little grey man with whom he had shared his food.

Simpleton told the little grey man all about his third task.

The little grey man said, "I have drunk the wine for you, I have eaten the bread for you, and I will also give you the ship because you were so kind to me."

This time, Simpleton did not have to walk back to the palace. He climbed into his ship and sailed off across the country.

When the beautiful ship sailed up to the palace, the king told Simpleton that he and the princess could be married straightaway.

Simpleton became a very good prince, and they were both very happy.

The golden goose had a special home in a corner of the palace, but no one ever saw the little grey man again.